GREAT ILLUSTRATED CLASSICS

THE
SECRET GARDEN

Francis Hodgson Burnett

adapted by
Malvina G. Vogel

Illustrations by
Shelley Austin Kaster

BARONET BOOKS, New York, New York

GREAT ILLUSTRATED CLASSICS

**edited by
Joshua E. Hanft**

Contents

About the Author

Born 1849, Frances Hodgson was from a wealthy English family. The death of her father and failure of the family business made the Hodgsons move to an American uncle's log cabin in rural Tennessee. Here Frances learned to love nature and gardening.

Frances loved to make up stories. As a teenager, she began writing them down and selling them to magazines in England and in America.

After she married Dr. Swan Burnett and had two sons, Frances continued to write, gaining fame and wealth.

Although Frances started by writing stories for adults, her friend, Louisa May Alcott, author of *Little Women*, encouraged her to write for children.

Little Lord Fauntleroy, her first children's novel, *A Little Princess*, and *The Secret Garden* have stayed in print for almost a century.

Frances spent her later years in New York being a "fairy grandmother" to her grandchildren. This, she said, was "much better than being a fairy godmother."

Just before her death at age 74, Frances Burnett said, "With the best that was in me I have tried to write more happiness into the world."

Generations of readers have found that happiness.

She Was an Orphan Now.

Chapter 1

Alone in a New Home

Ten-year-old Mary Lennox sat in the plush carriage with her hands folded tightly in her lap and her lips pressed together in an angry scowl. She was an orphan now, on her way to live with a rich uncle in England.

Mary's black dress and black hat made her look paler, thinner, and more sickly than she actually was. But Mary didn't care how she looked. Why should she? Her parents never did. They were dead now, dead from the terrible cholera epidemic that had spread throughout India, the hot country in Asia where Mary had been born and where she had been living for all of her ten years.

Her father, an official of the British Government ruling India, had always been too busy with his work to care about Mary. And her mother, who had never wanted a child in the first place, had been concerned only with going to parties with her friends.

Mary had been raised by her *Ayah*, the Indian nurse who obeyed her orders and gave the child everything she wanted except love. The result was that Mary Lennox was a selfish, spoiled little girl whose tantrums got her her own way with everything she wanted.

But now, the tall, stout, beak-nosed woman who sat opposite Mary in the carriage as it rumbled over the darkness of the English moor had no intention of giving the child everything she wanted. As housekeeper to Mr. Archibald Craven, the girl's wealthy uncle and only relative, Mrs. Medlock was not bothered at all by the girl's angry frowns and scowls, or

Raised by Her *Ayah*

by her refusal to talk.

Mrs. Medlock was simply following her master's orders—to go to London to meet the ship on which Mary was traveling to England in the care of a poor clergyman. However, she didn't expect the warning that Reverend Crawford gave her.

"My family took care of the child until we could arrange to bring her here. But I have to warn you, Mary's a difficult child to manage. Our own five children found her so disagreeable, they began calling her *Mistress Mary, Quite Contrary*, after the rhyme."

Now, as Mrs. Medlock looked at Mary, she felt a flicker of pity for the child who had been orphaned at such a young age, and she decided she'd better prepare her for what to expect. So she asked, "Did your mother or father ever speak to you about Misselthwaite or about your uncle?"

"No! My parents never spoke to me about anything. They never had time."

A Flicker of Pity

"Then, you'd better listen well. Misselthwaite Manor's a big gloomy place on the edge of the moor. Growing up in India, you probably don't know much about the moor, but it's a bare wasteland where not much grows and where sheep and ponies run wild. Mr. Craven's family built the Manor six hundred years ago. It's got a hundred rooms, though most of them are locked up. Outside, there are parks and gardens . . . and nothing else."

Mary had been listening even though she didn't want to show she was interested. So she wasn't prepared for Mrs. Medlock's sudden ending of "nothing else."

But the woman did continue. "As for your uncle, I'm certain he's not going to trouble himself about you. He doesn't trouble himself about anyone, not even—"

She stopped again, but took a breath and went on. "Your uncle's a fairly young man who was born with a crooked back. He always brooded about his back and hated his life and

A Gloomy Place on the Moor

his home until he got married. Mrs. Craven was a pretty young thing who truly loved him and didn't care a bit for his money. And he was so much in love with her that he'd have given her anything in the world she wanted. Then when she died—"

Mary had never felt sorry for anyone in her life, but she suddenly felt very sorry for her uncle.

"When she died, it made Mr. Craven hate his life even more than before. He doesn't care for anyone and won't see anyone. He's been spending the last ten years traveling all over the world. But even when he's home, he locks himself up in his wing of the house and won't let anyone in except his servant."

As if to make the gloomy story even gloomier, the rain began beating down on the carriage windows. Mary stared out, thinking, "A dreary day and a dreary story about a dreary house on a dreary moor!"

Still, Mrs. Medlock's voice droned on. "You'd

Mrs. Craven Was a Pretty Young Thing.

better not expect anyone at Misselthwaite to talk to you or play with you or look after you. There are plenty of gardens to play in, but inside the house, you'll be told which rooms you can go into and which ones you can't. Mr. Craven won't permit you to wander or go poking about the house."

"I don't care to poke about his house at all," snapped Mary, as her sympathy for her uncle disappeared just as quickly as it had appeared. Then, under her breath, she whispered, "If he's that unpleasant, he deserves everything that's happened to him!"

Mary turned her eyes back to the rain as it beat at the window. The noise of the carriage rumbling over the rough, rocky road was broken only by the wild, rushing sound of the wind howling around them. Inside the carriage, however, there was only silence.

On and on they drove through the darkness. After several hours, a light appeared in the distance and Mrs. Medlock breathed a sigh of

"I Don't Care to Poke About!"

relief. "That's Misselthwaite up ahead."

Trees on both sides of the road formed an archway leading up to a massive stone house. When the carriage stopped in the courtyard, a footman helped Mrs. Medlock and Mary down, and the girl followed the housekeeper to an enormous wooden door.

Once inside, Mary found herself in a huge hall. Family portraits hung on the walls, and suits of armor stood on the stone floor.

An old man servant approached Mrs. Medlock and said politely, "The master says you are to take the child to her room. He's leaving in the morning and doesn't wish to see her."

Mrs. Medlock nodded, then led Mary up a wide staircase, down one long corridor, then another, until she stopped at a door.

"This is your room," she said, opening the door and leading Mary inside. "This, and the one next to it, your nursery, are the only ones you're allowed to stay in. And don't you dare forget that!"

"The Master Doesn't Wish to See Her."

"I Hate It!"

Chapter 2

Martha

When Mary opened her eyes the following morning, she stared around the room, past the young maid cleaning out the fireplace to a large, deep window. "What's that?" Mary asked, pointing to the bare land that seemed to stretch endlessly beyond that window.

The young housemaid got to her feet. "It's the moor, Miss. Do you like it?"

"I hate it!"

"That's because you're not used to it. It's bare now, but you'll get to like it, especially in the spring and summer."

Mary stared at the plump, smiling girl who was perhaps only a few years older than herself and she said haughtily, "My servants in India bowed to me and obeyed my orders and wouldn't dream of asking *me* any questions. You certainly are a strange servant."

The girl laughed. "I know that, Miss. I'm just a common Yorkshire girl with no training. Martha Sowerby's my name. Mrs. Medlock, who's my mother's oldest friend, gave me this job out of kindness."

"Then are you to be my servant?"

"I'm Mrs. Medlock's servant, but I can wait on you a bit. Surely you're old enough so you won't need much waiting on."

"Who is going to dress me?"

Martha's eyes opened wide in amazement. "Can't you dress yourself?" she gasped.

"I never did it in my entire life. My *Ayah*, my Indian nurse, always dressed me."

"Then it's time you learned," said Martha, not realizing that she was being rather bold

"Can't You Dress Yourself?"

for a maid. "It'll do you good to wait on yourself a bit. My mother always says she couldn't understand how rich children didn't grow up to be fools after being washed and dressed by nurses all the time."

"How dare you call me a fool!" cried Mary in a rage. "You don't know anything about how servants are supposed to treat people!"

At that moment, Mary felt so helpless, so lonely, and so confused about this new life that she buried her face in the pillows and began to sob uncontrollably.

Simple, good-natured Martha felt sorry for her, and she went to the bed and patted the sobbing girl. "Don't cry, Miss. I didn't mean to upset you. And you're right, I don't know anything about how to treat people."

After a while, Martha's comforting words calmed Mary, and she said gently, "It's time to get up and have your breakfast, Miss. I set up your tray on the table near the fire. And I'll help you get dressed if you have any buttons

"Don't Cry, Miss."

in the back. I do it all the time for my little sisters and brothers. There's twelve of us children, you know."

Martha went to the big wardrobe and took out a white wool dress and matching coat. She held them up for Mary and said, "These are yours, along with lots of others Mr. Craven ordered Mrs. Medlock to buy for you. He didn't want you wearing black."

"I hate black and these *are* nicer."

As Martha began helping Mary into her new clothes, she continued chatting in her good-natured, friendly manner about her family and about how poor but happy they all were.

Once she was dressed, Mary sat down at the table, but pushed away the cereal when Martha tried to serve it. "I don't want it!"

"Don't want it!" exclaimed Martha in horror. "You can't let good food go to waste! Why, if my brothers and sisters were here, they'd have these plates empty in minutes."

"Why?"

"You Can't Let Good Food Go to Waste."

"Why? Because in all their lives, they've never known what it was to have their stomachs filled with food, that's why!"

"I've never known what it's like to be hungry," said Mary coldly and indifferently.

"Well, maybe it would do you good to be hungry once in your life. I've no patience with people who stare at food and waste it."

"Then why don't you take this food to your family?"

"Because it's not mine! And besides, it's not my day off either. I get off one day a month, just like the other servants. On that day, I go home and clean my mother's house so she can get some rest."

Mary took a few bites of toast and drank some tea, then walked to the window. She stood staring at the gardens and trees and paths that all looked dull and wintry. Then she turned and looked at the gloomy room.

"There's nothing to do today," she said with a sigh. "No one to play with me."

"No One to Play with Me."

"Why not go out? You'll have to learn to play by yourself. Children who have no sisters or brothers do. Even with our twelve children, my brother Dickon goes off to the moor and plays by himself. He's made friends with all the animals there—the ponies, the sheep, the birds—all of them."

Mary decided that seeing birds might amuse her, so she followed Martha downstairs and stood at the door as the girl explained, "There's lots of gardens here, with flowers and vegetables and orchards, but nothing's blooming now. There's walls and doors into all the gardens...except one. It's locked up. No one's been in it for ten years."

That made Mary curious. "Why would a garden be locked up?"

"It was Mrs. Craven's garden, and the master locked it up and buried the key when she died so suddenly."

Then, hearing Mrs. Medlock calling her, Martha hurried back inside the house.

"There's Lots of Gardens Here."

Great Walled Gardens with Built-In Doors

Chapter 3

A Ten-Year-Old Secret

As Mary headed down the walk, she passed huge old trees, large pools with fountains, evergreens trimmed into strange shapes, and great walled gardens with built-in doors. But all these doors opened easily when Mary tried them, so she knew they couldn't possibly be the hidden garden.

When the path she was following finally ended, she came to a very long wall. It, too, had a door in it. Since the door was open, she walked through it and found herself in a bare, ugly garden. Coming towards her was an old man with a spade over his shoulder. He tipped his cap politely to her, although the frown on his face showed that he wasn't at all pleased to see her.

But Mary wasn't pleased to see him either. "What are these gardens?" she asked coldly.

"The kitchen gardens, where we grow fruits and vegetables for the household."

"Can I go into all of them?"

"If you like, but there's nothing to see."

Mary went through a door into one garden, then into another and another, hoping each time that she'd reached the door to the mysterious locked garden.

When she came to the last one, she noticed that the wall seemed to extend beyond the garden and that tall trees lined the other side of the wall. On the topmost branch of one tree sat a bird with a bright red breast. He stared down at her for several minutes, then suddenly burst into song.

Mary listened to the song, feeling pleased

A Frown on His Face

that someone seemed to be paying attention to her. The lonely little girl almost smiled as she listened to his song. Then, when he was finished, he flew off.

"I hope you come back and sing for me again, little bird," she whispered. "Do you live in that tree? Is that tree in the hidden garden?"

On her way back, Mary found the same old gardener digging in a nearby orchard. He didn't look up from his work until she started talking about the robin. Then he gave a low whistle, and the next moment, the little bird was flying towards them.

When the bird landed on a pile of earth beside the gardener's foot, the old man chuckled and asked, "Is this your first visit to old Ben Weatherstaff this season?"

"What kind of bird is he?" asked Mary.

"Why, he's a robin redbreast, and the friendliest, most curious bird alive. I took care of him when he first flew out of his nest and was too weak to fly back. By the time his wings got

"I Hope You Come Back!"

stronger, the rest of his family had already flown off, so the lonely little fellow came back to me."

"I'm lonely also," said Mary.

"I guess I am too, Miss, except when he's with me. He's the only friend I've got."

"I don't have any friends at all," admitted Mary. "I never had anyone who liked me."

"Then you and I are very much alike," said Ben, sighing. "We both frown most of the time and probably have nasty tempers too."

Mary had never heard such truths about herself in her entire life. Her Indian servants would never dare criticize her, but she was beginning to realize that Yorkshire people, like Ben and Martha, were very honest and plain-speaking, and she began to wonder if she was as unattractive and nasty-tempered as Ben Weatherstaff said.

Suddenly, the robin's song interrupted her thoughts, and Ben exclaimed, "He's decided that he likes you and wants to be friends."

"I Am Lonely Too."

"With me?" asked Mary in amazement. Then, in a voice that was soft and eager, a voice that Mary Lennox had never used before, she asked, "Do you really want to make friends with me, little bird?"

The old man couldn't hold back a chuckle. "Why, you sounded just like Dickon does when he talks to his wild creatures on the moor."

Mary was about to ask Ben to tell her more about Dickon, but just then the robin flew up and over the orchard. "He's going into the garden with no door!" she cried.

"He lives there," explained Ben. "That's where he was hatched, among the old rose trees, and that's where he'll build his nest when he finds a mate."

"I'd love to see the rose trees," said Mary. "There must be a door somewhere."

"There was a door ten years ago, not now. Don't go poking your nose where it doesn't belong. Now, go back to your play, Miss."

"Go Back to Your Play, Miss."

Her Favorite Spot

Chapter 4

Mysterious Cries

As the days passed, Mary began spending most of her time outdoors, since staying inside the big old house meant doing nothing. Her favorite spot was a place on the long wall where the ivy seemed to grow more thickly than anywhere else.

One day while she was there, a chirp made her look up. It was Ben's robin calling to her to follow him as he hopped along the wall. Mary actually began to laugh as she ran after him, trying to chirp and whistle to him in his language. Suddenly, he flew up to the top of a tree on the other side of the wall.

"He's in the garden no one can go into," Mary said. "How I wish I could see it!"

Mary began running along the path, trying once again to find a door. But there was none. "There *must* have been one ten years ago if my uncle buried the key for it," Mary reasoned. And the more she thought about it, the more she was certain that she was right.

That evening after dinner, Mary asked Martha to stay and talk with her. She had a great many questions she was curious about.

"Martha, do you know why my uncle hated the garden?"

At first Martha hesitated, but when Mary insisted, she answered. "Mrs. Medlock has ordered us not to talk about that . . . and lots of other things too. But I *can* tell you that Mrs. Craven made that garden when they were first married and she loved it. They never let the gardeners tend to it, but did it all themselves. They'd spend hours there, planting or reading

"Mrs. Craven Loved the Garden."

or just talking.

"Their favorite place was an old tree with a branch bent like a seat. Mrs. Craven used to train the roses to grow over it and she'd sit there. But one day, the branch broke while she was sitting on it and she fell to the ground. She was so badly hurt that she died the next day. That's why the master hates the garden. He locked it up and won't let anyone go in or even talk about it."

Mary didn't ask any more questions, but in her young heart, she was suddenly finding out what it was like to feel sorry for someone other than herself.

Just then, a roaring sound interrupted Mary's thoughts about her uncle. "What's that noise?" she asked.

"It's the wind rushing round the house."

"Yes, I hear it, but I hear something else. It almost sounds like a child crying. And it's coming from inside the house."

Martha looked confused and nervous. "N-no,

The Branch Broke.

it's the wind on the moor," she stammered.

At that moment, a great rushing gust blew open the door to Mary's room, and the crying sound became louder and plainer than ever.

"There! I told you so!" insisted Mary. "It *is* someone crying and it isn't a grown-up!"

Martha hurried to the door and slammed it shut. "It *was* the wind," she stated firmly.

Something about the way Martha protested troubled Mary. She stared very hard at the young maid and thought, "I don't believe a word she's saying. It *was* someone crying!"

The next day, the rain was still pouring down in torrents. Once Mary had finished her breakfast and Martha had gone downstairs, Mary decided, "If I can't go outside and explore the gardens, then I'll explore the house instead. I'll count the doors and see if there really are a hundred rooms here and if they really are locked. Besides, no one much cares what I do or where I go anyway."

So, Mary opened the door to her room and

"It Was the Wind!"

went out into the corridor. She began wandering down the long corridor that branched into other corridors, then up a short flight of steps, which led to still other corridors and other flights of steps.

She opened doors and explored bedrooms; she studied portraits of Craven ancestors; she watched a family of baby mice cuddled up against their mother on a velvet sofa; and she played with a collection of tiny ivory elephants she found on a shelf.

After several hours of wandering, Mary decided to head back to her room. She lost her way several times, but at last was on her own floor, but not near her room. As she stood trying to decide which corridor to take, a cry echoed around her.

"There it is again, just like last night only closer! Now I'm sure it's a child's whine."

Mary turned towards the sound. It was coming from behind a tapestry on the wall. Suddenly, the tapestry parted and Mrs. Medlock

Tiny Ivory Elephants

came through it from another passage.

"What are you doing here?" she cried, grabbing Mary's arm and pulling her away.

"I turned the wrong corner and couldn't find the way back to my room," explained Mary. "And then I heard someone crying."

"You heard nothing of the sort!" snapped Mrs. Medlock. "Now come along back to your nursery or you'll be punished!"

Mary felt herself being pushed and pulled up one corridor and down another. Then she was shoved through the doorway of her room.

"Now, you stay where you're told or you'll find yourself locked up. I've got enough to do here without looking after you too."

Once Mrs. Medlock had slammed the door, Mary threw herself down on the bed, red with rage. Gritting her teeth, she insisted, "There *was* someone crying! There *was*! And I'm going to find out who or what it is!"

"What Are You Doing Here?"

"The Storm's Over."

Chapter 5

A Rusty Key Opens a Hidden Door!

Two days later, the rain stopped. Mary awoke to a sky bluer than any she had ever seen. She called to Martha, "Look! The storm's over."

"Storms do that during the night this time of the year. It's a sign that spring's on the way. That's when Yorkshire becomes the sunniest, most beautiful place on earth."

"Then I'm not going to stay indoors on such a beautiful day."

So Mary went out into the garden, where

Ben Weatherstaff showed her crocuses, snow-drops, and daffodils poking their tiny spikes up out of the earth. Then, when his friendly robin flew down to greet her, Mary asked Ben, "Do you think flowers are beginning to grow in the garden where *he* lives?"

"What garden?" snapped the old gardener.

"The one where the old rose trees are."

"Ask him," said Ben, pointing to the bird. "He's the only one who knows. He's the only one who's been inside that garden for the last ten years."

"Ten years is a long time. It's as old as I am," thought Mary as she left Ben and walked to-wards the Long Wall, as she had named it. She paced up and down in front of it, looking at the tops of the rose trees.

When the robin flew down and began peck-ing at the earth near her feet, Mary cried, "You do remember me! You do!" And she knelt down and began chatting happily with the bird.

He, in turn, sensed that Mary was his

"You Do Remeber Me! You Do!"

friend, and he let her come closer and closer until he was certain that she would follow him. He hopped to a small pile of freshly turned earth beside a hole that had claw marks from a dog's earlier digging.

Sticking out from the pile of earth was a rusty ring. Mary waited until the robin had flown back up to his rose tree, then she tugged at the ring.

"It's more than a ring!" she gasped. "It's an old key! It looks as if it's been buried for a long time. Can it possibly be the key to the hidden garden!"

Mary stared at the key in her hand for a long time, first in fear, then with excitement. "Now, if only I could find out where the door is, I could open it and go inside. Then I'd have a place of my very own to play in, a place where nobody would find me. I'll make sure that I carry the key with me always so that when I do find the door, I'll be ready!"

When Martha returned from her day off the

A Rusty Ring

following morning, she handed Mary a package and said, "I've brought a present for you."

"A present!" exclaimed Mary. "How could a family with twelve children to feed afford to give anyone a present?"

"A peddler came to our door, selling all sorts of things. Mother had no money to buy anything for herself or us, but when she saw a jump rope, she took some of the money I had given her from my pay and bought it for you. She wanted you to have something to play with."

Mary gazed in bewilderment at the jump rope. "Your mother is such a kind woman!" she exclaimed. "But I've never seen a jump rope before. How do you play with it?"

Martha ran to the middle of the room and began to turn the rope and skip into it, counting each skip until she reached a hundred. "Now you try it," she said, handing Mary the rope.

Mary's face shone with excitement as she took the rope and began to turn it. She was

"A Present!"

rather clumsy at first because her arms and legs weren't very strong, but she was determined to learn. So, when Martha suggested that it would be better to do it outside, Mary quickly put on her coat and headed for the door.

Just before she went out, Mary turned to Martha and said, "It was your pay that bought this jump rope for me. Thank you."

Those were strange words for Mary Lennox, who had never thanked people for doing anything for her and who had never liked people either. But now she liked Martha.

The sun was shining and a gentle wind was blowing as Mary skipped up one walk and down another, into one garden and out another, then on to her own special path along the ivy-covered wall. She had already counted up to thirty skips and was hot and breathless when she stopped to rest. She gave a little laugh when she spotted the robin swaying on a long branch of ivy in front of her.

Determined to Learn

"Yesterday, you showed me where the key was," she said to him. "So today, you ought to show me where the door is."

At that moment, the robin flew to the top of the wall and began to sing. Then a gust of wind blew along the path—a magical gust, Mary later swore. It blew aside several long vines of ivy, uncovering an iron plate with a doorknob and a keyhole set into it!

"It's the door!" she exclaimed. "The door that's been closed for ten years!"

Mary took the rusty iron key out of her pocket and pushed it into the keyhole—it fit! She gave it a slight twist—it turned!

Taking a deep breath, Mary looked around to see if anyone was coming, then she pushed open the door...slowly...slowly.

She quickly slipped through the opening and shut the door behind her. Standing with her back against the door, Mary looked all around her. "I'm here!" she gasped. "I'm inside the hidden garden at last!"

"It's the Door!"

"How Still It Is!"

Chapter 6

New Life in the Garden

The high walls of the garden were covered with thick brown stems of climbing roses, but there were no leaves or flowers on them. These stems also entwined themselves from branch to branch, connecting all the trees and bushes in the garden.

"How still it is!" Mary whispered as she began to walk around the garden. "And how mysterious! I must be the first person in here in ten years. The garden seems quite dead; there's not even a tiny bud anywhere. How I wish it were alive! . . . But at least I *am* inside and I can come here any time I choose. This can be my own special place."

Mary stopped before an alcove. At the base of it, the grass ended. "Why, there must have been a flower bed here once... and what's this?" She bent down and saw little green points sticking out of the black earth. "These must be the beginning of the flowers Ben Weatherstaff was telling me about. I wonder if there are more here."

Mary didn't know anything about gardening, but as she came upon more of these little points, she became concerned that the thick grass around them wasn't giving them enough room to grow. So she picked up a sharp piece of wood and for the next several hours dug out the weeds and grass until the ground around the buds was nice and clear.

"Now they can breathe," Mary said happily. "And I'll come back tomorrow and all the days after that to do the other beds too."

Looking down at Mary from his tree top, the

Digging Out Weeds

robin seemed to approve of his new friend and the work she was doing in his garden. After all, she was turning over the soil and uncovering all sorts of delightful things for him to eat.

Later, when Mary returned to the house for lunch, Martha was delighted. "Just look at your bright eyes, rosy cheeks, and huge appetite, Miss Mary! My mother will be so pleased to see what skipping rope has done for you."

"Oh, yes, Martha. I've been enjoying the rope. But there's something else I'd really like. Do you think I could get a spade?"

"Whatever for? What are you going to dig?"

"The house is so lonely, with no one to talk to except you and Ben, and you both have your work to do. I thought if I could buy a spade, I could ask Ben for some seeds and make my own little garden somewhere. Mrs. Medlock gives me a shilling each week from Mr. Craven, and I've saved five shillings so far,

Bright Eyes and Rosy Cheeks

since I haven't had anything to spend them on."

"Why, that's a fortune!" gasped Martha. "You can buy anything in the world with that. I saw a garden set in the village for two shillings, and the shop sells flower seeds too. Dickon knows which are the prettiest ones and how to make them grow. If you send him a letter, I'm sure he'd be happy to get the tools and seeds for you."

"Oh, Martha! You're such a nice girl!" Mary cried happily. "Then, when he has them, I can go to your cottage for them and meet Dickon and your mother too. I'd like that!"

Once the letter was written, Martha took it downstairs to have it delivered to Dickon by the butcher's boy, who was bringing an order to Misselthwaite.

When Martha came back upstairs, Mary was sitting cross-legged on the rug in front of the fireplace, looking at her curiously. Then she asked her a strange question.

"Send Him a Letter."

"Is the wind rushing around the house on a beautiful spring day like today, Martha?"

Martha was about to sit down beside Mary, but she stopped in surprise. "Of course not! Why do you ask that?"

"Because when you went downstairs to bring my letter to the butcher's delivery boy, I waited for you in the corridor. I heard that far-off crying again, just as we heard it the other night. You said it was the wind then, but there's no wind today."

"You mustn't go out into the corridor and listen for things!" scolded Martha. "Mr. Craven would be angry if he knew."

"I wasn't listening for anything. I was waiting for you and heard those same cries."

"I can't talk now, Miss Mary," said Martha as she turned to go. "Mrs. Medlock is waiting for me." And the girl hurried out the door before Mary could say another word.

"This is the strangest house anyone has ever lived in!" Mary whispered to herself.

"You Mustn't Go Out Into the Corridor!"

Clearing the Grass and Weeds

Chapter 7

Dickon

For the next week, the sun shone down on the Secret Garden, and Mary spent every waking hour clearing the grass and weeds. She worked steadily, never getting tired, and even seemed to gain more strength as the hours passed.

Each day on her way to the garden, she stopped to talk to Ben Weatherstaff and began to find the old gardener friendlier.

"If you had your own flower garden, Ben, what would you plant in it?"

"Bulbs, I guess, but mostly roses."

Mary's face lit up. "Do you like roses?"

"I do. A lady I once worked for taught me all about them. She loved all the roses in her own special garden. But that was over ten years ago, before she died."

"What happened to her roses? Did they die too once she wasn't there to care for them?"

"Well, I pruned the branches and loosened the earth around their roots once or twice a year. Some of them did manage to live."

But Mary needed more information. "When roses have no leaves, and look brown and dry this time of year, are they dead or alive?"

"You'll find out once the spring rain and sun fall on them."

"Do you go and see those roses anymore?"

"Not this year. My old bones are too stiff to—. Now, look here! Don't go asking so many questions! Go back to your playing!"

Mary went skipping away with her rope, a soft smile on her face. "He may be cross," she whispered, "but I really do like him."

"She Loved the Roses!"

THE SECRET GARDEN

As Mary skipped back toward the house through a wooded park, she heard a curious whistling coming from behind a tree. She approached the tree and discovered a red-headed boy about twelve years old sitting beneath it. His friendly face had big blue eyes and freckles. Seated around him were two rabbits, a brown squirrel, and a pheasant, all listening to the strange music he was making on a rough wooden pipe.

"Don't move," the boy whispered to Mary out of the corner of his mouth. "It will frighten them." Then he rose very slowly and added, "I'm Dickon Sowerby, Martha's brother. I know you're Miss Mary."

Mary didn't know anything about boys, so she asked shyly, "Did you get the letter?"

"Yes, that's why I came." He bent down and picked up a package from the ground. "I got you the garden tools and some seeds too."

Dickon unwrapped the seed packets and was about to start describing to Mary what

"I'm Dickon Sowerby."

they all were when a robin's chirping interrupted them.

"He's calling us," Dickon explained. "He
must know you and like you because those
chirps are the way he calls to his friends."

"Does he *really* like me?"

Dickon nodded and smiled. "He does. Now,
suppose we sit on this log and I'll teach you
how to plant your seeds. . . . But wait! It'd be
better if I *showed* you instead of telling you.
Where's your garden?"

Mary turned red, then pale. She didn't know
what to say. Did she dare share her secret with
him? Mary stared hard at Dickon for a minute,
then made an important decision. "Can you
keep a secret if I tell you one? A really important one?"

"I know where foxes have their lairs and
birds make their nests and rabbits dig their
holes, but I never tell the other boys. I can
keep secrets."

"Then listen! I found a garden. It isn't any-

"I Can Keep Secrets."

body's. Nobody wants it or cares for it. They're just letting it die."

"Where is it?"

"Come with me and I'll show you."

Dickon followed Mary to the ivy-covered wall. His big blue eyes opened wide in amazement as she pulled aside the thick green leaves and unlocked the hidden door.

As she led him into the garden, Dickon whispered, "It's a strange place, but very pretty. I never thought I'd ever see it."

"Then you knew about it?"

Dickon nodded. "Martha told me there was a garden, but that no one ever went inside."

"Look at all the roses! Are they dead?"

"Not all of them. Look!" Dickon held up a branch and told Mary, "This part is old and dead, but this green part is new and alive."

"That's wonderful!" cried Mary happily. "Let's see how many live branches are here!"

Dickon followed her eagerly, going from tree to bush, checking branches all around them.

"The Green Part Is New and Alive."

He explained things about plants that Mary had never known before, and both of them cried out with joy each time Dickon's knife revealed a live branch.

Suddenly, Dickon pointed to one of the little clearings Mary had made with her stick. "Who did that?" he asked in surprise.

"I did," she said proudly.

"You've done quite a lot of work for such a small and inexperienced girl," he said.

"I'm getting bigger and stronger, and I love to smell the fresh earth. There's a lot of work to do here, Dickon. Will you help?"

"I'll come every day if you want me to, rain or shine. Waking up this sleeping garden is the best fun I ever had in my life!"

"Dickon, you're as nice as Martha said you were. I like you. You make the fifth person I've grown to like."

"And who are the other four?"

"Your mother and Martha, and Ben Weatherstaff and the robin."

Both of Them Cried Out with Joy.

Dickon began to laugh. He laughed so hard, he had to cover his mouth so as not to be heard outside the garden walls.

Mary began to laugh too, then she asked him a question she had never dreamed of asking anyone before. "Do you like me, Dickon?"

"Yes, I do. I like you wonderfully well, Miss Mary, and so does the robin."

"Then that's two for me."

Just then, the noonday clock sounded in the courtyard and Mary said, "I have to go in for lunch. Do you have to go home too?"

"No, I carry my lunch with me." And he took out a little packet from his jacket pocket and unwrapped a bacon sandwich.

Mary hated to leave, but as she turned to go, she asked one last time, "Whatever happens, you'll never tell, will you?"

"Just as I'd never tell where a bird's nest is, I'd never tell about your garden either! Not ever!"

And Mary knew she could trust him.

"Do You Like Me, Dickon?"

"Dickon and I Are Going Planting!"

Chapter 8

A Sad and Lonely Uncle

"You're a bit late, Miss Mary," said Martha. "Your lunch is getting cold."

"That doesn't matter!" exclaimed Mary. "I've seen Dickon and he's wonderful and—"

"I know he's wonderful," chuckled Martha proudly. "I guess he brought you the garden tools and seeds."

"Yes, and Dickon and I are going to start planting right after lunch."

"I'm sure Ben would help you too. Mr. Craven lets him do pretty much what he likes because he was here when Mrs. Craven was alive and she liked him ever so much!"

Mary ate her lunch quickly and was about to go out again when the door opened and Mrs. Medlock came in. "Your uncle came back this morning, Mary, and he wants to see you in his study now, before he leaves again tomorrow. He probably won't be back until the fall or winter."

Mary turned pale. "He didn't want to see me when I first came. Why now?"

There was no reply, and Mary held her breath in fear as she silently followed the housekeeper down several corridors into a part of the house she had never seen before. "I know he won't like me," she thought, "and I know I won't like him either."

They entered a room where Archibald Craven was seated in an armchair before the fire.

"You can leave now, Mrs. Medlock," he said. "I'll ring when I'm ready for you to take Mary back."

Mary stood waiting, nervously twisting her

Mary Stood Nervously.

thin hands together. "He's not a hunchback at all," she thought. "He's just got high, bony shoulders. He really would be handsome if his face didn't have such a sad look."

"Come here, child!" said her uncle.

Mary timidly approached his chair.

"Are they taking good care of you?"

"Yes, sir. They're feeding me well too."

"I intended to send you a governess or a nurse, but I forgot. I'm sorry."

"No, please! Please—" Mary began, then sobbed, "I'm too big for a nurse, and I don't really want a governess, not yet."

"That's what Mrs. Sowerby said when she met me on the road. She said it would be better for you to play outdoors for a while until you put on weight and got stronger."

"She knows a lot about children," said Mary, gaining courage. "She has twelve. Her daughter Martha takes care of me here."

"Then what do you want to do, Mary? I know I'm a poor guardian for a child and I can't give

"Come Here, Child!"

you time or attention. But I want you to be happy and play wherever you like. Do you want anything? Toys? Books? Dolls?"

"M-may I have . . . a b-bit of earth to plant seeds in?" she stammered nervously.

"A bit of earth," he whispered, and his dark eyes looked at Mary with kindness. "You remind me of someone else who loved the earth and things that grew. Yes, child, if you see a bit of earth you want, take it and make it come alive with things that grow!"

"May I take it from anywhere if it's not being used?"

"Yes, of course, anywhere. . . . I'm tired now, child. You must go. I'll be leaving tomorrow and I'll be away all summer." Then he rang the bell for Mrs. Medlock.

When the housekeeper entered, he told her, "You need not look after the child too much. Let her do as she wishes in the garden. She needs to run about in the fresh air and get stronger. She may visit the Sowerbys too."

"Make It Come Alive with Things that Grow!"

Mrs. Medlock was pleased that she wouldn't have to "look after" Mary too much. But Mary was even more pleased as she burst into her room to share her news with Martha.

"I can have my garden!" she cried. "I can have it anywhere. And I can visit your cottage too! Isn't that marvelous!"

"Yes, it is! That was nice of Mr. Craven."

Then Mary became serious. "He really *is* a nice man, except that he's so sad and so lonely and frowns so much."

By the time Mary returned to the garden, she realized that Dickon would be gone. It was late and he had a five-mile walk back to his cottage. But there was a message stuck onto a rose bush. It was a picture of a bird sitting in its nest and below it, the words: *I will come back.* Mary understood that the drawing was Dickon's way of reassuring her that just as he kept secret the locations of birds' nests, he would also keep secret the location of *her* nest, her Secret Garden.

A Message Stuck onto a Rose Bush

Taking the Candle from the Nightstand

Chapter 9

A Secret Meeting

Springtime in Yorkshire brings unexpected weather changes, and that night Mary was awakened by torrents of rain beating down on her window and gusts of wind rushing around the corners of the house. No matter how hard she tried, she couldn't fall back to sleep.

After an hour of tossing and turning, a new sound made her sit up in bed. "That's not the wind! That's the same crying I heard before. I must find out what it is!"

Mary took the candle from the nightstand beside her bed and tiptoed softly out of her room. The corridor was long and dark, but she was too excited to be afraid as she headed for the place where the crying was coming from. When she reached it, she gasped, "It's the same passage, with the tapestry covering, that Mrs. Medlock came out of when I was exploring the house."

Mary turned into the passage and stopped in front of a door that had a glimmer of light beneath it. "Someone's crying in that room," she whispered. "A young someone."

Mary opened the door and stepped into a huge bedroom with lavish furniture and a big, glowing fireplace. The crying was coming from a thin young boy lying on a carved four-poster bed. His cries seemed to be cries of anger rather than of pain.

The light from Mary's candle made him turn his head on the pillow. "Who are you?" he asked as his huge gray eyes stared at her.

"I'm Mary Lennox. Mr. Craven is my uncle."

"He's *my* father! I'm Colin Craven."

A Thin Young Boy

"Your father!" gasped Mary. "No one ever told me he had a child. Why didn't they?"

"They didn't dare tell you because you'd have wanted to see me. I don't let anyone see me, *ever!*"

"Why?" asked Mary, puzzled.

"Because I'm always sick and I'll probably die soon, or if I live I'll be a hunchback."

"Don't you let your father see you?"

"Yes, but he usually comes when I'm sleeping. He doesn't want to see me because my mother died when I was born. I've overheard people saying he hates me. Once, I had to wear an iron brace to keep my back straight and that made people stare at me. But then an important doctor from London examined me and made them take the brace off. He told them what I needed was to be outdoors. But I hate the fresh air and won't go."

All the while he was talking, Colin kept staring at Mary, and it soon began to make her feel uncomfortable. "Why do you keep looking

"Once, I Had to Wear Iron Braces."

at me like that?" she asked.

"Because you seem like a dream. But if you are real, I want to hear all about you."

So Mary sat on a stool beside Colin's bed and began telling him about herself—her life in India, her voyage to England, and her days at Misselthwaite. She left out only the part about the Secret Garden.

Colin, in turn, explained about his life. "My nurse taught me how to read, and I read much of the time because I have nothing else to do. My father buys me anything I want, but nothing really amuses me. The servants must obey everything I ask because they know that if I get angry, I become ill. Besides, everyone is certain that I'll never live to grow up. By the way, Mary, how old are you?"

"Ten, just like you."

"How did you know that? I never told you."

"Because when you were born, the garden door was locked and the key was buried. It's been locked for ten years."

"You Seem Like a Dream."

Colin sat up, startled. Without realizing it, Mary had given away part of the secret. But Colin's curiosity was just as great as Mary's, and he began bombarding her with questions. "What garden door? Who locked it? Where was the key buried? Did you ever look for it? Did you ask the gardeners about it?"

Mary tried to answer those questions she could, but she had to tell Colin, "No one will talk about it. I think they've been ordered not to answer any questions."

"I could make them tell *me*. Everyone here must obey me. They all know that *if* I live, this place will belong to me one day."

"Why do you say *if* you live? Don't you think you will?"

"I don't think so. People have always been saying I won't. Besides, my doctor is my father's cousin, and if I die, he'll inherit Misselthwaite. . . . But let's not talk about that. I'd rather talk about the garden."

At this, Colin's eyes began to sparkle as he

Colin Sat Up, Startled.

went on. "I really want to see it, if we can find the key and dig it up, and unlock the door. I'll make the servants take me there in my wheelchair."

"No! No! Don't do that!" cried Mary nervously, fearing that everything would be spoiled if the servants knew. So she calmed herself down and reasoned with Colin. "If you make them open the door, they'll know all about the garden and it will never be a secret again. But if we could get inside without anyone knowing, we could play there every day and dig and plant seeds and make the garden come alive. It would be our very own secret forever!"

Colin dropped back on his pillow and his face took on a dreamy expression. "I've never had a secret before, except for overhearing the grown-ups say I wouldn't live. But I like this secret better."

"If you don't make the servants take you to the garden, I'm certain I could find a boy who

"I've Never Had a Secret Before."

could push your chair. Then it will always be our secret."

"I'd like that ... the fresh air ... the things growing in our Secret Garden."

Mary felt relieved. The idea of keeping a secret seemed to please him. So, she was surprised when Colin pointed to a curtain covering the wall above the fireplace and told her, "Pull the cord and open the curtain. Now I'll share a secret with you."

Behind the curtain was a painting of a beautiful young woman. Her big gray eyes were the same shape and color as Colin's, except that hers sparkled with laughter, while his were dimmed with sadness.

"She's my mother," Colin explained. "I don't know why she died, and I sometimes hate her for it. Perhaps if she had lived, I wouldn't always be so sick and my father wouldn't hate to look at me."

"Why do you keep her picture covered?"

"I don't want everyone else to see her, and I

"She's My Mother."

don't want her looking at me."

"Well, thank you for letting me see her," said Mary gently, "and for letting me see you too."

"I want to see you every day, Mary. Come to me and tell me how your search for the garden is going. But for now, I don't want anyone else to know that we've met. You'll be *my* secret, and I'll send messages for you with Martha. I can trust her."

"So Martha knows about you. That explains why she became so upset whenever I heard you crying and asked her about it."

"Martha waits on me when my nurse is off."

"And I'm here to help now too, Colin. But you look sleepy now. Suppose I pat your hand and sing you to sleep, just like my *Ayah* used to do in India. Would you like that?"

"That would be so nice," he said dreamily.

A few minutes of patting and singing put Colin into a sound sleep. Mary picked up her candle and softly tiptoed out of the room.

"Suppose I Pat Your Hand."

Martha Turned Red with Fright.

Chapter 10

Colin, the Young Rajah

The next day it rained and Mary had to stay in. She didn't get to see Martha until the afternoon, when the girl came up to the nursery after her chores were done. Mary greeted her excitedly.

"Last night, I found out what the sounds were. I followed the cries and met Colin!"

Martha's face turned red with fright. "You shouldn't have, Miss Mary! You'll get me in trouble because they'll think I told you about him and I'll lose my job. Then how will I ever help my mother?"

"You won't lose your job, Martha. Colin was glad I came and really enjoyed having someone to talk to."

"Are you sure?" gasped Martha. "You don't know what he's like when he's angry."

"He wasn't angry, I tell you. We talked and talked, and he even showed me his mother's picture. Then I patted his hand and sang him to sleep."

"I can hardly believe you! But if Mrs. Medlock finds out, she'll blame me for telling you and fire me immediately."

"Colin and I aren't going to tell her anything. It's going to be our secret for now. Besides, he says Mrs. Medlock and everybody else here must do what *he* wants. And he wants to see me every day. He'll tell you when to bring me."

"Me?" cried Martha. "Now I'll lose my job for sure!"

"You can't if you're just obeying his orders. But tell me, Martha, what's wrong with him

"It's Going to be Our Secret."

anyway? Do you know?"

"No one knows for sure. It seems that Mr. Craven went crazy when Master Colin was born because of his wife dying like that. I hear he wouldn't even look at the baby. He just raved that it was going to be a hunchback like himself and would be better off dead!"

"But Colin doesn't look like a hunchback."

"No, not yet. But everyone's always been afraid that his back was weak and would become hunchbacked. So they keep him lying down and don't let him walk. Once, they even made him wear an iron brace until a doctor from London made them take it off. He scolded Colin's doctor here for giving the boy too much medicine and letting him have his own way too much."

"He does seem to be rather spoiled."

"He's worse now than he ever was. It's true that he's been sick a lot, with colds and rheumatic fever and even typhoid."

"How awful for Colin!" gasped Mary. "Do *you*

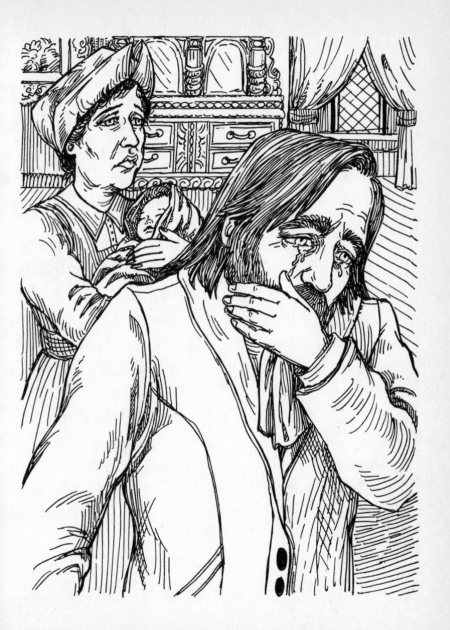

"He Wouldn't Even Look at the Baby."

think he's going to die, Martha?"

"My mother says he hasn't got much to live for if all he does is lie on his back and take medicine and refuse to get fresh air."

Just then, the bell rang and Martha said, "That's probably Colin's nurse wanting me to stay with him a bit so she can rest."

Martha wasn't gone more than ten minutes when she came hurrying back in, a puzzled expression on her face. "You must have bewitched Master Colin, Miss Mary. He's out of bed and on his sofa in a fine velvet robe, reading his books. He sent the nurse away until six o'clock, then told me, 'I want my cousin Mary here right now. And make sure you don't tell anyone!'"

Mary was delighted as she followed Martha to Colin's room. It was the first time she was seeing its bright pictures and colorful rugs and wall hangings in daylight.

Colin greeted Mary with a smile. "Come in. I've been thinking about you all morning."

Colin Greeted Mary with a Smile.

"I've been thinking about you too, Colin. But Martha, here, is terribly frightened that she'll lose her job because of this."

Colin turned to the servant girl and firmly said, "Martha, you and Medlock have to follow my orders, don't you?"

"Everybody has to, sir," replied Martha.

"Well, if she tries to send you away, I'll simply send *her* away! I can do that too!"

"Thank you, sir. I'll do my duty to you."

Once Martha had left the room, Colin turned to see Mary staring at him. "Why are you looking at me like that?"

"For two reasons. First, you remind me of a boy I saw in India. He was a Rajah, a prince, all dressed in silks and jewels. He spoke to his people just like you spoke to Martha, and they obeyed instantly or died!"

"A Rajah? . . . Hmmm. And the other reason?"

"I was thinking how different you are from Martha's brother, Dickon. He's not like anyone

A Boy I Saw in India

I've ever met. He can charm foxes and squirrels and birds by playing on his pipe, just like snake charmers do in India. But he doesn't call it magic. He just believes that because he's grown up with all these animals on the moor, that he's one of them. Don't you think the moor's a beautiful place?"

"I've never seen the moor or much else actually, because I'm always ill. And I'm sure I never will because I'm going to die."

Mary didn't like Colin's talk about dying. She had no sympathy for anyone who felt sorry for himself. "How do you know you're going to die?" she demanded.

"Everyone always says I will and they wish it too—the servants, Dr. Craven, and probably even my father!"

Mistress Mary was now feeling quite contrary. She stamped her foot and exclaimed, "Well, if they wished *I* would die, just to spite them, I wouldn't! And besides, I don't believe your father feels that way at all."

"I'm Going to Die."

Colin turned and stared at Mary. "You don't?" he asked in amazement. Then he leaned back against the sofa pillow, deep in thought for several minutes.

Finally, Mary broke the silence. "Did the doctor from London who took off your brace say you were going to die?"

"No, he simply told them that I would live if I kept my spirits up and made up my mind to live."

"I'll tell you who could keep your spirits up. It's Dickon. He always talks about living things, not dead ones. Let's talk about Dickon and the moor and his family and the things growing out of the earth now. *That's* talking about living, Colin."

And that's exactly what they did. They talked and listened. They laughed about things children laugh about and at times even laughed about nothing. They were laughing so hard and so long that Colin forgot about his weak back and actually sat up.

Colin Forgot about His Weak Back.

In the midst of all this laughter, the door suddenly opened and in walked Mrs. Medlock and Dr. Craven.

"Good Lord!" exclaimed the housekeeper.

"What is the meaning of this?" barked the doctor.

Mary stared at Colin and again saw the young Rajah seated majestically on the sofa, unconcerned over the two who had come in.

With a wave of his royal hand, Colin pointed to Mary and explained, "This is my cousin, Mary Lennox. I asked her to come here today and talk to me. I like her and want her here whenever I send for her."

Mrs. Medlock tried to clear herself of any wrongdoing. "Dr. Craven, I don't know how this happened. None of the servants would ever dare tell her about—"

"Nobody told her anything!" interrupted Colin. "She heard me crying and found me. I'm glad she did."

Dr. Craven looked angry, but he knew better

"What is the Meaning of This!"

than to go against the boy's wishes. He sat down next to Colin and felt the boy's pulse. "I'm afraid you've had too much excitement, Master Colin. You mustn't forget that you're ill and need to rest."

"But I *want* to forget that I'm ill, and Mary makes me do just that. There'll be lots of trouble for you if you try to keep her away," warned Colin, staring defiantly at the two grown-ups. "Now, Doctor, suppose you have my nurse bring up Mary's afternoon tea with mine. We'll have it together."

Bewildered and helpless, Dr. Craven and Mrs. Medlock looked from Colin to Mary, then turned and left the room.

Once the door had closed, the two children began to giggle, then laugh hard again.

"You were wonderful, Colin!" cried Mary.

"Yes, I was, wasn't I? Now, I want to hear all about the Rajahs in India since you have decided that I am so much like them."

The Two Children Began to Giggle.

They Read and Talked Together.

Chapter 11

Tantrums and Hysterics

Another week of rain gave Mary and Colin many hours together. They read and talked about Rajahs and gardens and Dickon and the moor. By the end of that week, Mary became convinced that Colin *could* be trusted with the secret about the Secret Garden. She also realized that taking him out to watch things grow might make him think less about dying.

Even Mrs. Medlock noticed a change in him and she told Mary, "Your time with Colin has been a blessing to all of us. He hasn't had a tantrum or whining fit since the two of you became friends." And for the first time, Mary saw the housekeeper actually smile.

When the rain finally ended and Mary awoke to a sunshiny day, her first thought was, "I can't wait! I must see the garden!"

She put on her clothes in minutes and was out of the house before anyone was awake.

"It's so different already!" she cried as she saw buds uncurling, grass much greener, and a sky the most beautiful blue. Clapping her hands in pure joy, she ran to the door in the Long Wall and entered the garden.

As she did, a shiny black crow flew down and alighted on an apple tree. Beneath the tree was a little red fox quietly watching a red-haired boy as he weeded and loosened the earth in a flower bed.

Mary flew across the garden, calling, "Oh, Dickon! How did you ever manage to get here so early? The sun rose only minutes ago."

"I knew that the moor and the garden would be alive and waiting for me after all the rain.

Clapping Her Hands in Pure Joy

And I've brought some friends with me too." He pointed to the little fox cub at his feet and the crow who had flown down onto his shoulder. "This little cub is Captain and my crow's name is Soot."

Both animals followed the children as they ran around for several hours, happily sniffing the warm spring earth and kissing the budding flowers.

When they stopped to rest for a while, Mary's face took on a serious look. "I have to talk to you about Colin," she said, then went on to tell Dickon about finding her cousin and their visits together all week. Finally, she asked, "Do you think Colin really wants to die?"

"No, but he probably wishes he'd never been born. He feels unwanted and so afraid of becoming a hunchback that he won't even try to sit up."

"He'll never get well with those gloomy thoughts in his head. But no one can be gloomy

"The Cub Is Captain, and the Crow Is Soot."

here, with everything so full of color. Perhaps if Colin came out here in his wheelchair, he wouldn't be talking about dying. We'd just be three children watching a garden grow. That would be better medicine than anything Dr. Craven gives him."

Mary and Dickon spent the rest of that morning working in the garden and planning for Colin's great adventure. When Mary returned to the house for lunch, she asked Martha to tell Colin she'd be working in the garden and would see him later that day.

Martha was frightened at delivering such a message. "It might put him in a bad mood."

"He can't have his way with everything. I'll see him when I get back!"

Mary didn't return until late afternoon and found Martha waiting in her room.

"I wish you had gone to see Master Colin," she groaned. "He's been having a tantrum all day, and none of us could quiet him."

"Well, he's got a nerve making such a big

Martha Was Waiting in Her Room.

fuss! I can do what I choose with my own time. I'll just tell him so right now!"

Mary stormed through the corridors to the boy's room. Colin was lying flat in his bed, facing the wall. "Why didn't you get out of bed today?" she angrily demanded.

"I did, this morning," he said, without bothering to look at her. "But when you spent your time with Dickon instead of with me, I went back to bed and decided I won't let him come here to see me, not ever!"

Mary flew into a rage. "If you send Dickon away, I'll never come into this room again!"

"You will if I order you to, you selfish thing!" he shouted.

"You're more selfish than I am!"

"Your Dickon's the selfish one, keeping you playing in the dirt and leaving me here all alone!"

"He's nicer than any boy I've ever known."

"He's just a common boy from the moor."

"He's better than a common Rajah like you!

"Why Didn't You Get Out of Bed Today?"

A thousand times better!"

"I'm *not* as common as you! And I've got a lump on my back and I'm going to die!"

"You are not!" shouted Mary. "You just want people to feel sorry for you!"

In spite of his weak back, Colin sat bolt upright in bed and threw his pillow at Mary. "Get out of this room!" he raged.

"I'm leaving," she screamed as the pillow landed at her feet. "And I'm never coming back. I *was* going to tell you all sorts of nice things about today, but now I'm not. You can stay in your room and never get any fresh air and die, if you like! It would serve you right!" And she stalked out the door without so much as a backward glance.

Mary returned to her room, feeling that some of the happiness of this day had been spoiled. But her spirits lifted when she found Martha waiting there with a gift from her uncle—a box of books and games.

"He remembered me," she whispered, and

A Gift From Her Uncle

her hard little heart grew warm. "The first thing I must do is write a thank-you letter to him." Then, as her heart grew warmer, she decided, "I know I said I'd never go back to Colin, but perhaps I *will* go in the morning, even if he throws his pillow at me again!"

Because she had been up since early that morning, Mary went to bed immediately after supper. It seemed like the middle of the night when she was awakened by terrifying screams and feet hurrying in the corridors.

"It's Colin having one of those tantrums!" she said, putting her hands over her ears.

Her terror lasted only a few minutes, then turned to anger. She jumped out of bed and stamped her foot. "He's got to be stopped!"

Just then, her door was flung open and Colin's nurse rushed in, gasping, "He's worked himself into terrible hysterics and might harm himself. No one can do anything with him. Will you try? He likes you."

Mary flew down the corridor, getting angri-

146

Terrifying Screams

er and angrier, till she burst into Colin's room. "You stop this instant!" she cried to the boy who was lying with his face down in bed and beating his pillow. "I hate you! Everybody hates you! I wish they'd all leave and let you scream yourself to death!"

The shock of hearing someone talk to him like that was the best thing that could have happened to Colin Craven. He turned over, gasping and choking. His face was red and swollen.

But Mary wasn't done yet. "If you scream one more time, I'll scream too, and I can scream louder than you and scare you!"

Colin was so startled that he actually stopped screaming. Tears began streaming down his face and he was shaking all over. "I can't stop! I can't!" he sobbed. "I felt the lump, I felt it! I'm becoming a hunch-back! I'm dying!"

"You didn't feel any lump, Colin. There's nothing the matter with your back, nothing at

"I Felt the Lump!"

all! Turn over and let me see it."

It was a poor, thin back that Mary examined up and down as she bent over her cousin as seriously as any doctor would. "There's not a single lump here," she said at last. "Not even one the size of a pin head. If you say you've got a hunchback one more time, I'm going to laugh at you! Even your nurse says that the London doctor told her you'd probably get well if you stopped having tantrums and got lots of fresh air."

Colin gulped as great tears streamed down his face. He smiled weakly and reached his hand toward Mary's. "I'd like to go out with you and Dickon. I'll go to sleep now, but you said you had so many things to tell me. I want to hear them. Did you find the way into the Secret Garden?"

"Yes," said Mary, staring at the tired little face and huge swollen eyes.

"Oh, Mary! If I could get into it, I think I really would live to grow up!"

"Not a Single Lump Here."

Colin Had a Fever.

Chapter 12

Children Need Children

The next morning, Colin had a fever and had to stay in bed. Mary stopped by to see him on her way out to meet Dickon and again when she returned. It was then that she told him, "Dickon will be coming to visit you tomorrow with all his animal friends."

"That's wonderful!" cried Colin.

"But that's not all," Mary whispered excitedly. "The rest is better.... I found the door leading into the Secret Garden!"

Colin's eyes opened wide and he gasped for breath. "Oh, Mary, does that mean I'll get to see it? Will I live to go inside it?"

"Of course you will! Stop being so silly!"

Then Mary began describing everything that was growing in the garden. Colin sat up and listened, fascinated. He forgot his aches, he forgot his fever, he forgot he was tired.

Mary knew the time had come to tell her cousin the whole truth. "Colin, I've been going into the garden for weeks now, but I didn't dare tell you before this. I wasn't sure I couldn't trust you with the secret."

"And you do now?"

"Yes, I do! Now, get out of bed and we'll sit on the sofa and look at the garden books together. Then I can point out which flowers you'll be seeing in the Secret Garden."

When Dr. Craven and Mrs. Medlock opened Colin's door a while later, they found, to their surprise, the two children laughing and chatting over their books.

Colin's laughter turned to a frown when he looked up and saw the doctor. Putting on his

Chatting Over Their Books

most important Rajah air, he announced, "I'm much better now and don't really need you, Doctor. In fact, in a day or two I'm going out in my wheelchair to get some fresh air."

Dr. Craven felt the boy's pulse. "Only if the weather's good and if you don't tire yourself. But your nurse will see to that."

"Fresh air won't tire me," stated the young Rajah confidently, "and Mary is going with me, and Dickon too, *not* my nurse!"

Dr. Craven shuddered. If this annoying boy got well, Misselthwaite would never be his. But the doctor wasn't an evil man and would never do anything to harm Colin. So, with a deep sigh, he said, "Mary seems to know how to care for you, and I know Dickon is a strong boy. So, you'll be safe with them."

As they turned to leave Colin's room, Mrs. Medlock said to the bewildered doctor, "It's just as Susan Sowerby said, 'Colin and Mary are just children. Children learn from children. Children need children!'"

"Children Learn from Children."

Mary Burst Into the Room.

Chapter 13

Visitors for Colin

When Colin awoke the next morning, he didn't stare at the walls and think about dying. Instead, his mind was full of wonderful things he'd be doing with Mary and Dickon and his animals, and the beautiful things they'd all be seeing in the Secret Garden.

He wasn't awake more than ten minutes when Mary burst into the room, her hair loose and blown and her cheeks pink from running in the fresh air.

"It's so beautiful out today!" she cried breathlessly as she ran to the window and threw it open. "Spring has come for sure!"

Mary went on to describe everything in the garden—the sweet-smelling breezes gently blowing the trees, the flowers uncurling, the birds singing, and the playful little animals Dickon had brought with him.

Colin was overjoyed as he listened, even to the point of ignoring his nurse when she brought up breakfast trays for him and Mary. However, he did let her put on his velvet robe and seat him on the sofa beside Mary.

Then, using his most Rajah-like manner, Colin announced, "A boy and a fox and a crow and two squirrels and a newborn lamb are coming to visit me this morning. I want them *all* brought up to me as soon as they come."

The two children giggled at the nurse's shocked face, but immediately attacked their food. When Colin had finished his entire meal, Mary sat back and smiled at him.

"You'll start getting fat soon, just as I did," she said. "I never wanted to eat when I was in

Attacking Their Food

India, but I always do now."

"I haven't been this hungry since I can't re-member when," replied Colin.

No sooner had the nurse taken away their trays than Dickon walked into the room. A newborn lamb was in his arms and Captain, his little red fox, trotted by his side. One squir-rel, Nut, sat on his left shoulder and Soot, his crow, on his right. Shell, his other squirrel, was peeping out of his jacket pocket.

Colin stared in wonder and joy as Dickon walked over to him and gently placed the new-born lamb in his lap. The little creature im-mediately nuzzled its body into the folds of Colin's soft velvet robe.

"What does it want?" he asked.

Dickon took a small bottle from his pocket and pushed the nipple into the lamb's mouth. "That's what, Master Colin. Now you can hold the bottle and feed it the rest."

While Colin stared in fascination at the tiny creature he was feeding, Dickon told him how

Colin Stared in Wonder and Joy.

he had found the lamb alone on the moor beside its dead mother and had wrapped it in his jacket and taken it home to feed and care for.

The other animals with Dickon had no interest in his story and chose instead to amuse themselves by exploring the room and the tree outside Colin's big window.

When the lamb had finished its bottle and was sound asleep on Colin's lap, all three children began looking at the pictures in the garden books. As Dickon named those flowers that Colin would be seeing in the Secret Garden, the boy's excitement grew.

"I'm going to see the snapdragons!" he shouted. "I'm going to see the columbines! I'm going to see them all! I'm going to be alive to see them all!"

"I'm Going to See the Snapdragons!"

Planning Colin's Trip to the Secret Garden

Chapter 14

"I Shall Live Forever!"

Another week of rain followed, but this time the children didn't mind. Dickon and Mary came to Colin's room every day, and the three spent their time making their plans for Colin's trip to the Secret Garden. They had to be certain everyone believed that he was going out with Mary and Dickon simply because he liked them and for the fresh air.

They planned their route, up one path and down another, across woods and around flower beds. They had to be sure they weren't seen after they turned a corner of the Long Wall.

When the day of their great adventure finally arrived, Colin sent for Mr. Roach, the head gardener. "I'm going out in my wheelchair this afternoon at two o'clock," announced the young Rajah. "If the fresh air agrees with me, I may go out every day. When I do, no one is to be out in the garden. I don't want anyone to see me."

Once Colin had dismissed Mr. Roach with a wave of his hand, as Mary said the Rajahs dismissed their servants in India, Colin leaned back against the cushions and smiled dreamily. "It's safe now. This afternoon, I shall see the Secret Garden! This afternoon, I shall be *in* it!"

Mary and Colin were so excited, they were barely able to eat their lunch. Once the nurse had dressed Colin, the strongest footman in the house carried him down to his wheelchair. Dickon waited as Colin's nurse tucked blankets around him, then the young Rajah dismissed her with a wave of his hand.

Dickon pushed the chair slowly and steadi-

Carrying Colin Down to His Wheelchair

ly down the path, as Mary walked beside it. Colin leaned back and lifted his face to the sky, breathing in the sweet-smelling air, gazing at the puffs of snowy white clouds, and listening to the singing of the birds and the humming of the bees.

Even though no gardeners were in sight, the children followed their mysterious route just for the fun and excitement of it. When they turned into the long walk by the ivy-covered wall, they began to whisper.

"This is where I used to walk up and down and wonder and wonder," Mary explained.

"But I can't see any door," whispered Colin as he eagerly searched the ivy vines.

"Just wait."

They went a little farther on, and Mary pointed again. "This is where the robin showed me the key."

Colin leaned forward. "Where? Where?"

"And this, Colin, is the ivy that the wind blew back," said Mary as she lifted the thick

Following the Mysterious Route

green leaves.

"Oh, there it is! There's the handle and the door!" gasped Colin, and he covered his eyes with his hands and held them there.

"Quickly, Dickon!" whispered Mary. "Push him in!"

With one strong, steady push, the chair was inside the Secret Garden.

Colin fell back against his pillow as the wheelchair stopped. He dropped his hands from his eyes and slowly looked around. Vines of green leaves covered the walls like a carpet. Splashes of purple, white, and pink blossoms covered the trees and bushes. Wings fluttered above the boy's head, and the sun gently warmed his thin, young body.

A pink glow suddenly spread across his face, and Colin Craven, the boy who was convinced that he would die, cried out, "I shall get well! I shall get well! And I shall live forever and ever and ever!"

"I Shall Get Well!"

To Look at, Touch, and Smell

Chapter 15

A Wonderful, Magical Day

Dickon and Mary moved Colin's chair under a plum tree whose snow-white blossoms formed a canopy that belonged in a fairy tale book.

"I feel as if this spring day was made perfect just for me," said Colin dreamily as Mary and Dickon brought buds and twigs and leaves and bird feathers from the ground for him to look at and touch and smell.

"Do you think we'll see the robin today?" asked Colin.

"You will, after a while," said Dickon. "He's

finished building a nest for his mate and their young, and he's pretty busy carrying worms to them."

The afternoon was filled with new, happy things every minute with only one exception. That was when Colin spotted an old gray tree with no leaves on it and asked, "Is it dead? It looks as if a big branch has broken off."

Dickon and Mary looked at each other without speaking. They had already decided that if Colin asked about the branch, they would never tell him the truth about how it had broken ten years ago.

Finally, Dickon simply said, "That branch broke off a long time ago. Even though the tree is dead, the climbing roses have grown up over its branches and will be blooming soon. Then the dead wood will be covered."

Just then, Dickon spotted the robin and he looked up with relief. "Look, Colin! There he is, the robin you've been looking for."

And Mary thought, "There must be magic at

"There He Is, the Robin."

work here today, sending the robin at this moment to distract Colin from that tree."

By the time the afternoon sun had begun to fade and his face had grown rosy from the fresh air, sunshine, and excitement of his new discoveries, Colin lay back in his chair and announced, "I don't want this day to end. But I'll come back tomorrow and the day after and the day after that. I've seen the spring and I'm going to see the summer. I'm going to see things grow and I'm going to grow myself."

"And we'll have you walking and digging with us before long, too!" added Dickon.

"Walk? Dig? Do you really think I can?" asked Colin in disbelief.

Neither Dickon nor Mary had ever asked if anything was wrong with Colin's legs, but Dickon bravely answered the boy's question.

"Of course you'll walk! You've got two legs like everyone else, haven't you?"

"Yes, and there's actually nothing wrong with them," admitted Colin. "It's just that

"I Don't Want This Day to End."

they're so thin and weak that I've always been afraid to stand on them."

Both Mary and Dickon heaved a sigh of relief. Then Mary firmly told Colin, "When you stop being afraid, you'll stand on your legs, and I think that's going to be soon."

They all sat thinking about that for a while until Colin suddenly pointed to the high wall and called out, "Who's that man?"

Dickon and Mary jumped to their feet and looked up. There was Ben Weatherstaff's angry face glaring at them from the top of a ladder outside the wall.

Ben shook his fist at Mary and shouted, "You've got no right poking your nose where it doesn't belong—"

Mary shouted back, "It was *your* robin who led me here, Ben Weatherstaff!" And she started walking towards him.

"How did you get in here?" he demanded.

"I can't tell you while you're shaking your fist at me!"

Ben Weatherstaff's Angry Face

At that moment, the gardener's fist froze in mid-air and his jaw dropped open as he stared over Mary's head at a boy sitting like a young Rajah in a luxurious wheelchair as it was being pushed towards him.

As the chair stopped under Ben's nose, the Rajah demanded, "Do you know who I am?"

Ben Weatherstaff stared as if he had seen a ghost. He gulped, then shakily replied, "Yes, I do. I recognize your mother's eyes staring out at me from your face. But how did you come here? You're a cripple."

Colin sat bolt upright, forgetting all about his weak back. "I'm *not* a cripple!"

"He's not!" shrieked Mary.

Ben's hands shook. His mouth shook. His voice shook. "Y-you haven't got a crooked back or crooked legs?"

"No!" shouted Colin. And suddenly the anger that he usually threw into his tantrums filled him with a strength he had never known before. He began to tear away the blankets

"I'm Not a Cripple!"

that covered his legs and he shouted to Dickon, "Come around in front!"

Dickon was in front of Colin in a second.

Mary caught her breath and whispered, "He can do it! He can! I know he can!"

Dickon held onto Colin's arm as the boy stretched out his thin legs and stood upright on the grass. He was standing as straight as an arrow, with his head thrown back and his eyes flashing fire!

"Look at me!" Colin yelled to Ben Weatherstaff. "Just look at me!"

"He's as straight as I am!" called Dickon. "As straight as any boy in Yorkshire!"

Tears began to stream down the old man's cheeks. He clapped his hands for joy and cried out, "Those folks all lied! You're as thin as a board, but there's not a lump on you anywhere. You'll live and grow up to be a man yet. And may God bless you!"

"This is my garden and you are my servant, Weatherstaff," said the young Rajah, standing

"He's as Straight as I Am."

up straighter and taller as the minutes passed. "You are never to say a word about what you've seen here today. Get down from your ladder and Mary will bring you in through the door. We didn't want you to know our secret, but we have no choice now."

Once Mary had left the garden to get Ben, Colin turned to Dickon. "Mary was right. I *can* stand. When I stopped being afraid, I did it! And now I'm going to walk to that tree." He pointed to a tree a few feet away and added, "I want to be standing when Ben Weatherstaff comes into the garden. I can lean against the tree if I need to."

Colin walked to the tree and though Dickon was holding his arm, he was wonderfully steady. He was standing there, straight and tall, when Ben entered with Mary.

Under her breath, Mary was whispering, "You can do it, Colin! I told you you could! Oh, Colin, you *can*! I know you can! Don't give in, not in front of Ben Weatherstaff!"

"You Can Do It, Colin!"

Then Colin took charge. "Look at me, Ben Weatherstaff!" he ordered. "Am I a hunchback? Have I got crooked legs?"

"Not you!" said the old man tearfully. "But why have you been keeping yourself shut in all these years?"

"Because I thought I was going to die. But now I know I'm not!" he said firmly.

"*You* die?" Ben said tenderly. "Nothing of the sort! You've got too much spirit and spunk in you. When I saw you put your legs on the ground in such a hurry, I knew you were all right. Now, sit down on your blanket, Master Colin, and give me your orders."

Colin agreed to sit for a while. "What do you do around here, Weatherstaff?" he asked.

"Anything I'm told to. They keep me on because your mother liked me."

"My mother!" exclaimed Colin. Then his gaze slowly circled the garden and he said quietly, "This was *her* garden, wasn't it?"

"Yes, sir, and she loved it very much."

"You've Got Too Much Spirit and Spunk in You."

"Well, it's mine now and I'm going to come here every day with Mary and Dickon. They worked to make it come alive, and now I will too. I may send for you sometimes to help us, but no one must ever see you come."

Ben's face twisted into a smile. "I came here for eight years to prune the roses, and no one saw me. I got in over the wall since I didn't know where the door was. But in the last two years my old back wouldn't let me climb over the wall and jump down."

"Why did you continue caring for her garden after she died?"

"Your mother was a pretty young thing, my boy, and she once said to me in secret, 'If I'm ever ill or go away, Ben, you must take care of my roses.' When she died, the Master ordered everyone to stay out of here. But I didn't. I came in. I followed *her* orders."

"I'm glad you did, Ben," said Colin. "I'm certain that you can keep our secret too!"

"Yes, sir. And it'll be easier on my back to

"You Must Take Care of My Roses."

come in through the door than to climb up over the wall."

Colin looked down at the grass beside him. Mary's trowel was laying there. He picked it up, and his weak hand began to scratch at the earth with it. Then he dug the trowel in and turned over a lump of earth.

Dickon, Mary, and Ben looked on silently, proud of what the boy had accomplished today and what he was trying to do now.

"You told me you'd have me walking and digging, Dickon," said Colin, "and I've done both today."

"How'd you like to plant something, Master Colin?" asked Ben. "I have some roses in pots in the greenhouse that you can plant right here in the ground."

"Oh, yes, please! I'd like that so much!"

Ben hurried off, forgetting his weak back. Dickon took a spade and began digging the hole deeper for Colin, while Mary ran to get a watering can.

He Dug the Trowel in.

When the two returned, Ben loosened the plant from its pot and handed it to Colin. "Here, lad. Set it in the earth, same as a king does when he visits a new place."

Colin's hands shook a little as he set the rose plant into the ground and held it upright as Ben patted the earth around it.

"It's planted!" said Colin. "Help me up, Dickon. I want to be standing when the sun goes down on this wonderful, magical day."

And whether it was magic or Mary's prayers or Dickon's strength, when the sun slipped down over the horizon, Colin was standing on his two feet—laughing and crying at the same time.

"There's magic here—good magic!" whispered Colin.

And Mary wondered if that magic might have had something to do with Colin's mother watching over him from Heaven.

"There's Magic Here—Good Magic!"

"Magic is Right Here in this Garden."

Chapter 16

Play-Acting

The idea of magic kept Colin awake most of that night, thinking and planning. To him, the best magic was that he had really stood on his feet. As he told Mary and Dickon and Ben in the garden the following day, "I'm convinced that if you tell yourself 'Nice things are going to happen' and you really believe it, magic *will* happen. Magic is right here in this garden. Mary and Dickon believed I could stand up, and I came to believe it too. I tried and I *did* stand.

"From now on, I'm going to tell myself every

day. 'There's magic in me that will make me strong and make me walk and make me live to be a man.' I'll begin by telling myself, 'I'm going to walk around the garden.' You three may follow behind me."

So with Mary and Dickon on either side for the young Rajah to lean on, and Ben and the little animals trailing behind, the procession began moving slowly but regally around the garden. They stopped to rest every few yards, but Colin kept his head held high and looked very grand.

"The magic's in me!" he kept saying. "The magic is making me strong. I can feel it!" And he wouldn't give up until he had led his little procession around the entire garden.

"I did it! It worked!" he cried.

"What will Dr. Craven say?" asked Mary.

"Nothing!" stated the young Rajah. "He'll say nothing because he won't know. He'd only tell my father and no one, not even my own father, will know my secret until I'm so strong

A Procession

that I can walk and run like any other boy. I'll work at it in the garden all summer, then in the fall when he returns to Misselthwaite, I'll walk into his study and say, 'Here I am, sir. I am like every other boy and I shall live to be a man!'

"Then he'll be proud to look at me, proud that he's got a son who's as straight and as strong as any other father's son. But we must be certain that the servants don't suspect anything. I'll still act like a weak invalid in the house and come here every day in my wheelchair. That should work."

Throughout the months ahead, the magic continued for the children. Magic in the roses coming alive. Magic in the new blooms each day. Magic in the animal stories Dickon told them. And even magic in the children's play-acting.

Colin and Mary had trouble holding back their laughter in front of the servants. The boy would scold the footman for not carrying him

Magic in the Children's Play-Acting

gently down the stairs, and Mary would pretend to pity her cousin with words like "My poor Colin!" or "Dear, weak Colin!"

By the time they got to the garden, Mary and Colin would burst out laughing so hard that often neither could catch their breath!

With each passing day, Colin's appetite increased from being out in the air and exercising. Both he and Mary were putting on weight, but getting hungrier by the minute. They couldn't figure out how to get more food at mealtime without arousing the doctor's suspicions or prompting questions by the servants. Mary even offered to let Colin eat her share, but he refused, telling her, "We must get fat together!"

Dickon came up with a solution, or rather his mother did, for the children had agreed to let the trustworthy Mrs. Sowerby in on their secret.

"When you go to the garden each morning," Susan Sowerby told Dickon, "I'll give you a

"My Poor Colin"

pail of milk and some currant buns for Colin and Mary. That way, they won't be so hungry when they return to the house at mealtime. Play-acting may be filling their hearts with joy, but we can't forget about filling their stomachs either!"

Though Mary and Colin were thrilled with Mrs. Sowerby's feasts, they knew how poor the family was, with fourteen mouths to feed. So they insisted on giving Dickon some shillings with which she could buy the food.

As the days went by, Colin walked more and more and became stronger and stronger. Dickon helped by showing him some exercises for strengthening the muscles in his arms and legs. Colin became convinced, without a doubt, that his magic was truly working!

Along with the new exercises that Colin and Mary did together, came even greater appetites for both children. Soon the buns and milk weren't enough to fill them up. Dickon solved this problem by bringing eggs and pota-

New Exercises

toes to the garden and roasting them in a little hole they dug in the earth.

This gave Mary and Colin another chance to play-act at the house by refusing some of the cook's fine dinners. It also gave Colin the chance to confuse the doctor by stuffing himself with food some days and eating very little on others.

Mrs. Medlock was just as confused as Dr. Craven when she saw the children gaining weight although they were eating very little. But she admitted to him that the additional weight was actually making Mary a pretty child. "Her hair has grown thicker and her face is all nice and rosy-cheeked. And she smiles most of the time now, and laughs, too, especially when she's with Master Colin."

"Laughter is fine for the children," said the doctor. "Let them laugh."

"Let Them Laugh."

Long Corridors and Empty Galleries

Chapter 17

A Mother Is Watching

Rainy days soon became a problem because Colin was too impatient to lie still on the sofa and pretend he couldn't move. He wanted to exercise the magic that had entered his arms and legs, but he couldn't be seen doing it inside the house.

Then Mary had an inspiration. "There are a hundred rooms in this house that no one ever goes into," she told him. "I found them one rainy day when I went exploring. There are long corridors and empty galleries where you could run and we could do our exercises and explore all sorts of rooms."

"It sounds almost like another Secret Garden!" cried Colin. "Let's go look at them. You could wheel me in my chair."

From that day on, rainy days became exciting days for Colin and Mary. Once the footman had carried Colin's chair either up or down the stairs, wherever they wanted to go, he was ordered away. Then Colin would bolt from the chair and run and jump from one end of the corridor to the other. When his running and jumping were done, he and Mary would do their exercises together, then explore the rooms containing family portraits and treasures hundreds of years old.

One afternoon, when Mary came to call for Colin, she noticed something different about his room. The picture above the fireplace was no longer covered by the curtain.

Colin saw her staring at it and explained, "Last night, I felt the magic in the room. It made me open the curtain and keep it open. I

Something Different About His Room

wasn't angry at my mother anymore. She wasn't laughing at me. She was laughing because she was glad to see me standing."

"You look so much like her now, Colin. Maybe her ghost is inside your body."

"No, if that were so, my father would like me. Perhaps he *will* like me one day. Then I'll tell him about the magic. That might cheer him up."

Once the rains were over, the children returned to the garden, where much work needed to be done. After several hours of weeding and digging, Colin suddenly dropped his trowel and stood up straight and tall. His face seemed to be glowing and his eyes were sparkling.

"Mary! Dickon! Look at me!" he called. "I suddenly remembered how weak my hand was when I tried to use this trowel my first day in the garden. And look at my hand now! I'm well! *I'm well!* I shall live forever and ever and ever, and I'll never stop making mag—Wait!"

"Mary! Dickon! Look at Me!"

He looked across the garden at a woman in a long blue cloak entering through the door. "Who's that coming in here?"

"It's my mother!" said Dickon happily.

All three children hurried to greet Susan Sowerby. Colin reached out his hands and smiled lovingly. "I've wanted to see you ever since I met Dickon. I've never wanted to see anyone or anything before."

"Oh, dear lad," she sobbed, touched by Colin's words, "how you startled me! You look so much like your dear mother."

"Do—do you think that will make my father like me?" the boy stammered.

"Oh, yes! He must come home and see you! You're standing so straight and tall, and your legs are fine and strong." Then she turned to Mary. "And you, dear lass, you've filled out so wonderfully. I'm certain that you'll grow up to be as pretty as I hear your mother was."

Mary didn't think she was pretty; she knew she looked different now than when she first

"It's My Mother."

came to Misselthwaite. But she was secretly pleased at the idea that she might some day look like her beautiful mother.

The children showed Mrs. Sowerby everything they had done in the Secret Garden and everything that was growing now. Colin felt so close to her that he even shared his thoughts about magic with her.

And she shared her feelings with him. "You must never stop believing in your magic, Colin, for it means believing in yourself. I tell that to my children all the time. Just ask Dickon."

Mrs. Sowerby had brought a feast for the children, and after their walk, she unpacked it on the grass under the big plum tree. As the children ate, she told them stories and made them laugh. And they made her laugh with their stories of the play-acting they were doing at the house.

"You won't have to keep it up very much longer," she told them. "I'm certain that Mr.

"Never Stop Believing in Your Magic!"

Craven will be coming home soon."

"Do you really think so?" asked Colin hopefully. "I can't wait to tell him all that's happened to me. I couldn't bear it if anyone else told him first. I've been planning all different ways of telling him for such a long time."

"I'd like to see his face when you do," said Mrs. Sowerby gently.

When it was time for Susan Sowerby to go up to the house for tea with Mrs. Medlock, Colin came up to her and put his hand in hers. He looked into her eyes adoringly and said, "You are just what I imagined a mother would be like. I wish you were my mother too, as well as Dickon's."

Susan Sowerby leaned down, her eyes wet with tears, and she hugged Colin to her. "Dear lad," she said, "I believe that your mother is here, right now, watching over you with her magic in this very garden."

"Dear Lad!"

A Bubbling Stream in Austria

Chapter 18

"In the Garden!"

While the Secret Garden was coming alive and two children were coming alive with it, Archibald Craven was traveling throughout Europe, just as he had been doing for the past ten years. He had been trying to forget his terrible sorrow, but running away from Misselthwaite Manor had never lifted his spirits before and it didn't now.

Once, he found himself sitting beside a bubbling stream in Austria when a clump of blue forget-me-nots caught his eye. For a few minutes, he actually let their beauty enter his thoughts and push his misery out.

"I almost feel alive again," he whispered to himself. "How can this be happening?"

It wasn't until months later that he would learn that on this very same day, at the very same hour, in a garden at Misselthwaite Manor, Colin Craven was shouting, *"I am going to live forever and ever and ever!"*

Archibald Craven's misery, however, returned the next day, and he continued his wanderings. As summer turned to autumn, his wanderings took him to Lake Como in Italy, where memories of Misselthwaite began crowding into his thoughts.

One night, as he sat in the rose garden of his villa, staring at the lake, a calmness began to creep over him. It crept deeper and deeper into his body until he fell asleep . . . and began to dream . . . and dream. But was it a dream or was it real? he wondered afterward.

In the dream, the happy, sweet voice of his dead wife was calling to him. *"Archie! Archie!*

The Happy, Sweet Voice of His Dead Wife

Come to me!"

"Lilias, my dearest! I'm coming to you!" he cried. *"Where are you? Where are you?"*

"In the garden! In the garden!"

Then the dream ended. But Archibald Craven didn't waken. He slept soundly in his chair beside the lake until the following morning, when he was awakened by his servant carrying a tray with the day's mail.

As he opened his eyes, Craven remembered the dream and he whispered, *"In the garden!* But the door is locked and the key, buried!"

Archibald Craven looked down at the letter on top of the pile. It was addressed in a woman's handwriting and had a Yorkshire return address. He opened it and read:

"Dear Sir:

My name is Susan Sowerby, the neighbor who once stopped you on the moor to speak to you about your niece, Mary. I know I'm being bold again by writing to ask you to please come home. You would be happy if you did. And if

Remembering the Dream

you will excuse my saying so, sir, I think your
wife would be asking you to come—if she was
here.

> *Your obedient servant,*
> *Susan Sowerby."*

Mr. Craven read the letter twice, with the dream still in his thoughts. Then he made a decision. "I will return home at once!"

A few days later, in his carriage crossing the moor, Archibald Craven let his thoughts wander to the boy he had been trying to forget for ten years.

"I remember how I behaved like a madman when Colin was born, because he was alive and his mother was dead. At first, I refused to even look at him. Then when I did, he was so weak and wretched, I was sure he would die. But he didn't. As he grew, his eyes became exact duplicates of his mother's and I couldn't bear to look at him. So I went into his room only when he was asleep.

"Can I make it up to him now or is it too

"I Behaved Like a Madman."

late? Was that Sowerby woman warning me that he's dying or telling me I could help him?"

As these memories came back to him, Archibald Craven was "coming alive." The magic was working on him, though he didn't know it yet. He only knew that his heart felt warm as his carriage approached Misselthwaite, a warmth he hadn't known upon returning home for ten years. And the words *"In the garden! In the garden!"* kept repeating in his head.

When he entered the house, he immediately asked Mrs. Medlock, "How is Master Colin?"

"Well, sir, he's—different, and none of us can figure him out. He used to eat nothing, then he developed an enormous appetite, then stopped eating again. He used to refuse to be taken outdoors, then suddenly insisted on going out every day, from morning to evening, with Miss Mary and Dickon Sowerby."

"How does he look, Medlock?"

"He seems to be putting on weight, sir. But

"How Is Master Colin?"

we're puzzled over his strange laughter when he's alone with Miss Mary."

"Where is Master Colin now?"

"In the garden, sir, though no one is allowed to know exactly which one, since no one is allowed to see him outdoors."

Archibald Craven heard only her first three words: *In the garden.* And he repeated them, *"In the garden!"* again and again until he was shouting them. Then he jumped up and ran from the room and out of the house.

His feet took him across the wide lawns and directly to the long walk, a path he hadn't traveled in ten years. He slowed down as he approached the high wall covered with thick green ivy. He remembered where the door was, but didn't know exactly where he had buried the key.

When he reached the door and was about to pull the ivy away, he stopped and listened. Strange sounds of running feet seemed to be coming from the garden, along with even

He Approached the High Covered Wall.

stranger sounds of children's voices trying to whisper and muffle their laughter.

"Good Lord!" he cried. "Am I dreaming? Am I hearing things? Am I losing my mind?"

And then the voices were shouting and the laughter was no longer muffled as the running feet came closer to the garden door.

The next instant, the door was flung open and a boy burst through it at full speed, without seeing the man he almost ran into.

Archibald Craven reached out his arms to keep the young runner from crashing into him, then stared at the boy in amazement. He was a tall, handsome lad, glowing with life and health. The boy's shiny dark hair had blown away from his forehead, and his large gray eyes with thick black lashes looked up at the man.

"W-who? W-what?" gasped Archibald Craven.

This was not the reunion with his father that Colin had been planning, although win-

A Tall Handsome Lad

ning the race ahead of Mary had delighted him. But he took control of the situation and, drawing himself up as tall as he could, he said, "Father, I'm Colin. You probably can't believe it, but I am."

"In the garden! In the garden!" whispered Archibald Craven dreamily.

Colin didn't quite understand what his father meant, so he tried to explain the changes in him. "Yes, it was the garden that did it. The garden and the magic and Mary and Dickon. No one knows I'm well. I wanted to keep it a secret until you came home and I could be the first to tell you."

The words came tumbling out in a rush. Then when Colin stopped to catch his breath, he reached out for his father's arm and said, "Aren't you glad, Father? Aren't you glad? I'm going to live forever and ever and ever!"

Archibald Craven's eyes filled with tears as he pulled his son into his arms and held him close. "Take me into the garden, my boy, and

Pulling His Son into His Arms

tell me all about it," he sobbed. "Tell me every-thing."

Mary and Dickon, who had followed Colin out the door and had been watching the re-union, went back into the garden with them.

Archibald Craven stood silent, just as the children had done, as he looked around the garden bursting with the golds and purples and reds of autumn flowers and leaves. "I thought everything would be dead," he said.

"Mary thought that at first also," said Colin. "But then everything came alive, Father, just as I came alive too."

Dickon, Mary, and Archibald Craven sat down under the plum tree, but Colin insisted on standing as he told the story of mystery and magic, of his first meeting with Mary, of Dick-on's animals, of his first visit to the garden, of getting out of his wheelchair to defy Ben Weatherstaff, of his and Mary's play-acting, and of all the secret things they had been doing for many months.

"Tell Me Everything."

Archibald Craven laughed until tears came to his eyes. And sometimes tears came to his eyes when he wasn't laughing either.

When Colin came to the end of his story, he declared proudly, "Now it doesn't have to be a secret anymore. I'm sure it will send everyone in the house into fits when they see me, but I'm never going to sit in that wheelchair again. I'm going to *walk* back to the house with you, Father."

All the servants had been watching at the windows since the Master had run from the house looking for Colin. Now, what they saw almost popped their eyes out of their heads.

Across the lawn came the jubilant Master of Misselthwaite. On one side of him, Mary and Dickon were skipping along, pushing an empty wheelchair. And on the other side, was Master Colin Craven, his head held high and his eyes full of laughter, walking proudly, as strong and as steady as any boy in Yorkshire or as any boy in all of England!

Pushing an Empty Wheelchair